COFFEE IS MY CALLING

A SHORT PREQUEL

BARRINGTON SERIES

SUSAN MACKIE

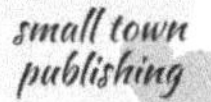

Dear Readers

I hope you love reading my stories as much as I love writing them. It's all for you. It really is.
I thank you, all of you.

Happy Reading,

Susan

THIS ONE IS FOR YOU, READERS

As an Independent author and publisher, moving from exclusive (Amazon only) to wide (all retailers AND my own website) has been a big decision and not without its challenges.

Many readers asked for my ebooks - the Barrington Series - to also be available from retailers such as Kobo, Apple, Google and Barnes & Noble and directly from my website.

Taking a deep breath, I booted up my new website in August 2023 - loading my books to it, and the wide retailers.

With beating heart and bated breath, I await the results. It's all about readers. Finding readers, connecting with readers. Writing for readers.

I thank those already enjoying my books, and those yet to discover my stories.

FOREWORD

While the town of Barrington exists, it is little more than a small village with a general store, hall and school.

I've imagined elements of nearby towns, such as Gloucester, to create the township of Barrington for this story.

Any similarities to people, living or deceased, are purely co-incidental and a product of my imagination.

The Barrington Tops, Bucketts Mountain, Barrington and Gloucester Rivers are real, and it is a stunning region to visit.

1

———

As the plane banked to the left, Debbie Webb peered through the small window, then leaned back slightly so the gentleman in the seat next to her could see. The magnificent Sydney Harbour had turned on its charm with the early morning sunshine glinting off the water, and a glimpse of the Opera House sails and the Harbour Bridge behind. Picture postcard perfect.

The most beautiful harbour in the world. Home after five years. Why had she stayed away so long?

She smiled as her flying companion drew in a breath. He'd told her earlier, during the dinner service, that it was his first trip. Coming to visit his son and a new grandchild. Flying into Sydney never failed to impress.

Working her way through luggage collection and customs, she admitted that landing meant she was on home soil. Australia. But Sydney wasn't really her home, although she had studied there years ago. No, she had a three-hour train trip ahead of her. She wouldn't be *home* until she stepped onto the platform at Barrington.

Finally, her luggage piled up on a cart, she was ready to make her way to the train. She'd change lines at Central, then an hour's wait. Straightening her shoulders, her backpack already heavy, she regretted for a moment not accepting her parents' offer to pick her up from the airport. But the return trip was long, and she knew they hated driving in the city. Shrugging to herself she pushed her trolley, piled high with five years of belongings, out through the crush of people waiting for loved ones to arrive. Her flying companion was just ahead, and tears came to her eyes when she saw him swept up in a younger man's hug, his wife standing beside him holding a small baby. Happiness radiated from the group which made her wish, again, that she had someone waiting for her.

Through the waiting throng, heading for the exit,

she heard someone shout, 'Debbie! Deb! Wait!' Turning, she peered toward the sound. Her name was called again, and she stood on tiptoes. There he was - head and shoulders taller than most of the crowd.

Greg Tait.

Their eyes locked. He was before her in three large strides, scooped her into his arms and swung her around in a circle. A giant of a man, his bulk made her feel like a small girl.

Laughing, she batted him lightly. 'Put me down Greg. Now!' Back on her feet, she glanced past him, wondering if he was alone.

'It's just me, young Deb. Little brother called me last night, said you were flying in. I was heading home for a few days anyway. I, er, have two weeks off.' These last words were said quietly.

'Oh. Really? What have you done Greg Tait?' Hands on hips she frowned at him.

'Just a little scuffle in yesterday's game. Pleaded guilty and I'm out for two.' He grinned, turning on his considerable charm. 'But good timing, eh Deb?' He winked.

'Indeed. But if what I've been reading in the paper is true, you might be permanently on the bench if you keep this up.' She stepped aside as he took over her trolley. People were watching them.

'That's Greg Tait. Rugby's bad boy!'

'Who's the girl?'

'Is she the assistant coach's wife? You know, the one he was …'

Greg pushed the trolley forward, smiling and waving at those staring, while keeping an arm slung around Debbie's shoulders as he moved forward.

Debbie wanted to shrug his arm off, but he was kind to pick her up. Yet she was aware he was probably using her as a decoy to put to rest the stories circulating in the press. She'd read about him in London, the day before her flight. The article discussed, not just his current alleged affair, but all the indiscretions and altercations in his ten years of professional rugby, with several teams. Described as a talented player in the early days, now more of a loose cannon. If the article was true, soon there wouldn't be an A Grade team that would have him.

As they exited the terminal, the heat hit her hard. She stopped, shrugged out of her jacket, slipping it into her oversize carryall. Greg's car was the latest Holden Commodore, looking more like a racing car than a sedan. But the interior was leather, the air conditioning cool and Greg's choice of music suited her mood. She stayed awake, asking Greg how Jamie and their parents were, until they crossed the Harbour Bridge. Three hours later they drove slowly through Barrington, finally arriving at her childhood home.

2

———

Jamie scooted out from under the tractor, wiped the oil from his hands, then checked his watch. Debbie's flight had landed, and she should be starting the journey home with Greg.

He wiped his face with an old cloth, took a swig of water, then rolled back under the tractor. If it hadn't broken down last night he would have picked her up himself. *Wanted* to pick her up. He sighed. But having his big brother do it was the next best thing.

He wondered how long Debbie was staying, she was vague in her texts. He'd loved her for years. Since they were sixteen. But after school their lives took different paths. He stayed to work the farm with his father as Greg was already playing rugby in Sydney, he'd been selected before he finished high school. Jamie had been a talented player too, and he knew selectors had checked him out in his last year at school. But by then Greg had a reputation in the sport. A good player, no, a *great* player, but hard to control. Jamie knew he played well too, good enough for the league, but there was a taint on his name. For a while he'd been disappointed, especially when Debbie went to Sydney to study. But now, ten years had gone by, and he was settled in Barrington and loved the farm. So much, that he was ready to take over completely, but his father was waiting for Greg to finish with football and come home to the farm too. Jamie's hand slipped and the spanner took the skin off his knuckle. He swore under his breath. While Greg always said he'd come back when his rugby days were over, Jamie secretly doubted he would. Or perhaps he secretly hoped he wouldn't. He loved him, sure. But it was easier to love Greg from a distance. He always brought a certain amount of chaos with him, and Jamie's own personality was quieter, more grounded.

Tightening the last nut, he slid out and sat up,

checking the time. *They'd be home now.* He'd go up to the house, call Debbie, see if she'd like him to drop in. She'd be tired from the long-haul flight, but he hoped she wanted to see him as badly as he wanted to see her. If she was only home for a few weeks, he wanted to be with her as much as he could. He hoped to convince her to come home permanently, but he wasn't sure she was ready for that.

He'd flown over last winter, when it wasn't as busy on the farm, and spent three weeks with her. Debbie had taken ten days off work, and they'd travelled through England, Wales, and Scotland together. They'd been close and it was all he could do not to tell her he loved her. He didn't want to pressure her into coming home, he wanted it to be her decision. Although a fully qualified physiotherapist, it was her second job that she'd talked about most. Working in a coffee shop in Notting Hill. She'd taken on so many hours there, that she barely worked more than twenty a week in her 'real' job at the hospital. He loved the way she lit up when she talked about changes she'd suggested to the owner, and how he'd made her a shift manager. He'd asked, as he was leaving, if she would come home soon, have another look at Barrington. Consider coming back permanently. Debbie had hugged him then, and he could feel her heart racing against his chest. She'd agreed, said she needed to visit her parents, even though they'd been to see her in London twice. But he hoped she was really coming to be with him.

Back at the house, he called her family home on the landline. Her Mum, Rachel, answered, her voice bubbly.

'Oh Jamie, you've just missed your brother. Greg brought Debbie home from Sydney. So lovely of him. We've had afternoon tea and he's on his way to you.'

'Thanks Rachel, yes, it was good of him.' Jamie paused. 'Um, is Debbie there? May I have a word?'

'Sorry Jamie, she's gone to have a shower and a nap. But I'll ask her to call you back.' Rachel's voice became muffled, he heard *in the fridge Steve, yes, that's right* – then she spoke into the phone again. 'And get Jill to call me, we'll have a barbecue while she's home, and Greg's here too.'

'Barbecue. Yes okay, I'll ask mum to call you.' Jamie nodded at Rachel's response and hung up, disappointed he hadn't been able to speak to Debbie. He turned around, his mother stood at the sink, filling the kettle. She looked at him, her face a mixture of sympathy and knowledge. She'd already told him she didn't think Debbie would return to

Barrington to settle, she'd travelled and worked overseas and would be used to city life now.

'Call Rachel back Mum, they want to have a barbecue. For Debbie.' He hoped his face didn't divulge his disappointment. 'And while Greg's here.'

3

Already second guessing her decision to permanently leave London, Debbie hadn't yet told her parents. She knew her Dad would be happy to have her back in the country, but she rather thought her Mum liked telling people *our Debbie works in London* and she definitely liked taking trips to see her, then travelling on to Europe. It may have been hard to get her Dad to leave Australia otherwise.

She'd kept in touch with Jamie all these years, never really letting go of her first love. But she'd dated in Sydney, then London. One relationship, with a medical intern, had lasted almost two years. It was fun, the relationship progressed quickly, and she moved in with him after three months. But when her parents visited, it all changed. Her mum adored Jason, but her Dad asked her what she was doing, did she think he was *the one?* And when she thought about it, she knew she was never going to marry him, she was just moving through the motions of having a grown-up relationship with someone that was more of a friend, than a love interest.

Then Jamie had called last year, seemingly out of the blue, and said he was coming to London, could they catch up. And that's when she knew. It was Jamie all along. She'd given him her heart at sixteen, her virginity at seventeen. And she loved him still. She'd heard he'd had a relationship for a while, with Melanie Mitchell. Debbie had gone to school with Melanie and hadn't been close to her. She always seemed to chase after the older boys, or men. When Jamie broke up with Melanie, she was pregnant, but she said the child wasn't his. He'd been hurt. Melanie had cheated on him. But at least she didn't try to pass the child off as his. She'd moved to Sydney after that, was probably married now with more children.

What she really needed was to see Jamie. Now. Walking into the kitchen, her mum was on the phone. Debbie put the kettle on and pulled two cups out of the cupboard. Using hand gestures, pointing to the kettle and teapot, she asked her mum if she wanted a cup of tea.

Smiling and nodding at Debbie, Rachel spoke into the phone again, 'Alright Jill, tomorrow night works. We'll do the salads, drinks and desserts and you'll bring the meat. At six? Perfect, see you then.'

Walking across to Debbie, her mum passed her the tea cannister, then gave her a quick hug. 'It's lovely to have you home.'

'Thanks Mum, I'm really happy to be home. I've missed it here. You and Dad, this town.' Debbie was about to say *Jamie* but paused.

'Oh, it must be funny to be in tiny little Barrington after the excitement of London!' Rachel had a dreamy look on her face. 'We love London. Our visits have been just fabulous. Next time we might go across to Spain after seeing you, we haven't been there yet.'

'Next time?' Debbie poured water into the teapot, her face turned away for a moment.

'Yes. Maybe next year, during our winter. I've been working on an itinerary.' She lowered her voice. 'Still trying to talk your dad into it, he says he wants to travel more around Australia now, but we can do that anytime.'

Debbie drew in her breath, about to speak, but her father walked in, a package in his hands.

'How are you feeling love? Tired?' he placed the parcel on the counter and gave her a kiss on the cheek. Debbie could smell pastries. He'd been to the bakery then.

'I'm good Dad, thanks. I slept most of the way here in the car. Happy to be home.' She took another cup out of the cupboard. 'Tea?'

'Yes thanks love. I picked up a little something for afternoon tea.' Grinning, he pointed to the package he'd just set down.

Rachel nudged him with her shoulder. 'What did the doctor say about pastries Steve?'

'One won't hurt. We're celebrating our girl coming home.' Winking at Debbie, he slid onto a high chair at the kitchen counter.

Debbie poured the tea. 'What *did* the doctor tell you Dad?' She pushed the cups towards her parents, sitting together. Studying her Dad for a moment, she realised he'd lost a bit of weight since his visit last year, but otherwise looked well. Her mum looked great, a few years younger than her Dad, she wasn't even sixty yet.

'My sugar was up a bit and my cholesterol too. Not enough for medication, I'm controlling it by diet.' He patted his stomach. 'I've lost five kilos and feel quite fit. For an old bloke.'

'You're not old!' Debbie and Rachel spoke in unison, then laughed.

'So nothing to worry about?' Debbie sipped her tea.

'It could have been, but we've nipped it in the bud.' He wrapped an arm around Rachel's waist. 'We've got places to go, things to see. We're living our best lives, now I'm fully retired.'

Rachel turned to Steve. 'Jill and Ross and the boys are coming for a barbecue tomorrow night. With Debbie and Greg both home, it seemed a good excuse to get together.'

Steve finished his tea and stood. 'Good. We haven't caught up for ages. I'll check the gas bottle for the barbecue. It was getting low last time.' He turned to Debbie. 'What are you going to do now?'

What she really wanted to do was see Jamie. 'Is there anything you need me to do Dad? Mum?'

'No love. Why don't you go for a walk down the street. There's been some changes since you were home.' Steve walked toward the back door, then turned around. 'You won't believe what they've done with the bank. You know they closed the branch just after I retired. We've still got two banks in town, but it's a shame.'

'Oh, I didn't know.' Debbie was sympathetic. Her father had worked at the branch his entire career and was the bank manager for the last fifteen or so years. 'What have they done to it?'

'Douglas Barlow, the solicitor, bought it. He has his office upstairs in what was the original manager's residence. Downstairs has been turned into two tenancies. The smaller one is a gift shop cum florist, and the other one is untenanted. He's put in a shell for a potential coffee shop or restaurant, but it's been sitting empty for six months. It's a small town, I'm not sure it could support another coffee shop. There's the bakery of course, then the burger place further up, and now we have a Thai restaurant as well as counter meals in the three pubs.'

Debbie's interest was piqued. An empty coffee shop, right here in Barrington! She'd been thinking about working in one, or at one of the pubs, if she stayed. Maybe try to get a bit of physio work at the hospital. But an empty shop. She wanted to run right out and have a look, but still hadn't told her parents she was home for good. 'Thanks Dad, I may go for a walk, stretch my legs a bit.'

Her father had left, and she was washing up with

her mum, when Rachel spoke. 'Gosh, Deb. I forgot to tell you. Jamie phoned while you were in the shower. Can you call him back?' She took the tea-towel from Debbie's hand. 'Although he's coming tomorrow night, so you'll see him then.'

'I'll give him a call back anyway. Thanks Mum.' Debbie walked back to her room. She needed to get an Australian sim card for her phone. Should have done that at the airport, but Greg's appearance had surprised her. She'd walk down the street, could pick one up from the supermarket.

4

———

Jamie stepped inside, it was cool after the heat of the machinery shed. He found Greg and his parents sitting on the back veranda, the men sipping on a beer. Greg sprang up, leapt at Jamie, putting him in a head-lock before messing his hair with his other hand.

'Little brother. You've got to think a bit quicker!' Greg and his dad laughed. Jamie was annoyed. He'd been working on the bloody tractor all day, his brother could have changed his clothes and helped.

'Piss off Greg.' He extracted himself, walked to the bar fridge and picked out a beer, then opened it, taking a large slurp. He flopped down on the veranda floor, his back against the railing. He wouldn't sit on his mum's pretty cushions while he was covered in grease and oil.

'Boys.' Their father's tone held a warning.

'Come on mate, where's your fighting spirit?' Greg's voice was teasing, but Jamie suspected he was aware that he could have been helping and hated being caught out.

'No fighting spirit here. Mate. I'm hot, I'm dirty and I'm thirsty. So I'm having this beer.' He took another big gulp. 'Then a shower and clean clothes. Then I'll see if Debbie's got time to catch up.' He looked at his brother, who had returned to his chair, a fresh beer in his hand. Looking at the empties on the table between he and his dad, he'd already had a few. His father wasn't a big drinker, maybe two at most for him.

'How was Debbie when you picked her up?' Jamie tried to keep his voice neutral.

'She's a gorgeous girl Jamie. Even sexier than she was at high school.'

'Greg! Stop it!' Jill looked shocked. 'That's a very disrespectful remark. Debbie is a lovely girl.' She looked from Greg to Jamie. She knew his feelings for Debbie.

'Joking Mum. Just trying to get a rise from little brother.' Greg narrowed his eyes as he spoke, and

Jamie had to take a breath to stay calm. It seemed every time he saw Greg lately, there was tension between them. It was a mistake to ask him to pick Debbie up, but the alternative was the train for her, and Jamie knew how tired she'd be from the flight.

'I'll see her for myself. And Mum's right. Don't speak about Debbie like that. She's not a football groupie.' Jamie finished his beer, placed it in the bin by the fridge, and stalked inside to get cleaned up.

He checked his mobile phone, not sure if Debbie would call there or the landline. Maybe she was still resting.

Ten minutes later he was in clean jeans and checked shirt. He'd drive over to Debbie's. If she was resting he could have a chat with Steve. But he hoped she wasn't resting.

Starting his Ute, he was just backing out when his phone rang. Unknown number. He almost didn't answer.

'Hello?' He knew his tone was suspicious, so many scammers called these days.

'Jamie! It's me, Deb. Just bought a new sim card, so this is my Aussie number now.'

Just hearing her voice made his mouth dry and his heart pound. 'Debbie! Great to hear your voice. Where are you?'

'Don't laugh. I'm in the pub across the road from the bank. Dad's old bank.' She laughed and Jamie's mood rose another notch. 'Had to get out of the house for a moment, stalking my old haunts.' She stopped. 'Where are you?'

'In my car, about to drive to your house.' He laughed out loud. He felt lighter. Happier.

'Come here instead.' She giggled. 'I'm on my second glass of wine. Can't wait to see you.'

'Ten minutes. Don't move an inch.' Jamie put the phone down, shifted into gear and was about to drive off when a tap on the window startled him. He wound it down. Greg. 'What's up?' Jamie was keen to get going.

'Where are you going bro? I'll jump in.' Greg started to walk around to the passenger door.

'No!' Jamie shouted from the window. 'Stay here. I'll see you later!'

He accelerated away. There was no way he was taking Greg with him. Jamie wanted Debbie to himself. And Greg had already had too much to drink. He looked in the rear mirror as he drove away. Greg was standing there, staring at him. He wasn't happy.

5

———

Debbie smoothed her maxi skirt down and fiddled with her hair as Jamie walked through the door. His eyes met hers and he was with her in a couple of strides. Tall, like his brother, but not as broad across the shoulders, Jamie still took her breath away. He'd been a skinny kid, not tall at all, through most of high school, then around fifteen he shot up and filled out. A lot of her friends had crushes on him in those days, but he had only ever sought Debbie out. She stood as he wrapped his arms around her, the top of her head just reaching his shoulder.

'Deb. I've missed you.' His simple, heart-felt words brought tears to her eyes.

Her face still against his shoulder, she sniffled,

then whispered, 'I've missed you too Jamie. So much.' They stayed that way, holding each tightly, for ages, until Bob behind the bar called out. 'Jamie. Mate. Order a drink. Please.'

They laughed, releasing each other. Debbie found a tissue, wiping her eyes carefully, while Jamie walked to the bar. He came back with another wine for her, and a glass of something for himself.

Debbie nudged him, jerking her head toward his drink. 'What's that?'

'Ginger beer. I had a real beer before I left home.' He slid onto a bar stool at the high table near the window beside her. 'I don't need alcohol to enjoy this. You're all I need.'

They sat together for a moment, neither speaking. She breathed him in. Clean-man scent. She wanted to put their drinks to one side and just kiss him. For a long time. Instead, she gazed across the road at the old bank.

'Big changes over there, eh?' Jamie pointed to the bank. 'Built in the late eighteen hundreds, solid building. They'd been wanting to close the branch for a while, I think. Then your Dad taking early retirement seemed to be the catalyst for it. It's a handsome old building. I haven't been upstairs to Barlow's, but mum says it's beautiful. High ceilings, ornate plaster, original fireplaces. And you know Frances Barlow will have it looking just right.'

'And downstairs? I had a quick look in the gift shop before they closed. It's lovely.' Debbie pointed to the other side of the front door. 'And Douglas has set this side up for a coffee shop, or restaurant, but he hasn't found a tenant yet?'

'Looks that way. I've heard locals talking about it. You know what they're like here. They're saying there's no market for another coffee shop. But I don't know. Tourism is increasing. If it was done right, not another burger café, something a bit more like the ones in the laneways of Melbourne, I think it would do alright.' Jamie took a sip of his drink, turning his gaze from the window back to Debbie. Her thick honey coloured hair swung over one eye as she turned her head. She pushed it back impatiently. Her nose was pert, and her luscious mouth very kiss-able. He'd always loved her grey eyes, so wide and expressive. She was beautiful. Perfect.

He took her hand, holding it against his chest for a moment. 'There's a barbie at yours tomorrow night. But I suppose you know that.'

'I do. Mum wants to celebrate me being home.' She giggled. 'And Greg.'

'Greg?' Jamie frowned.

'Mum seemed a bit excited to see him. I think she's a fan. He hugged her and she got all flustered.' Debbie cleared her throat. 'It was a bit embarrassing actually. I think Mum thought Greg, was, er, interested.'

Jamie was horrified. 'Interested in your Mum?'

'No! Not mum. Me, silly.' Debbie grinned and looked at him, the laughter dying on her lips. He was furious.

'What?' She reached her hand out to him.

'Bloody Greg! Thinks he can have whatever he wants! Used to getting whatever he wants!' A muscle in his jaw clenched.

'Whoa there cowboy. Firstly, I don't think Greg's interested in me at all. He's a notorious flirt and just... I don't know. Opportunistic.' She said the last word with a slight sneer and saw Jamie's face lighten. 'And secondly. The only Tait man I've *ever* been keen on is the one holding my hand right now. Jamie.'

His expression cleared. 'Sorry Deb.'

'Don't turn into a neanderthal now Jamie Tait. You've always been one of the good ones.' She spoke lightly, leaned in, and kissed him on the cheek. She took a deep breath.

'I want to tell you something. I haven't told mum and dad yet, you're the first to know.'

He set his drink down, gave her his full attention. She hoped her words wouldn't freak him out.

'I'm staying. I've quit my jobs in London. I'm home for good.' She waited, holding her breath, and was rewarded by the grin spreading across his face.

'Really?' He pulled her closer, kissed her hard and fast on the lips. 'May I ask why? Why now?'

She frowned. He seemed happy but wanted to know why. She paused, started to say something about it just being time to come home. Then stopped. If there was a chance with Jamie. A real chance, then she needed to be honest.

'The real reason, Jamie Tait, is because I want to be with you. Here, in Barrington. I've travelled and worked away, and I've learned a lot. But the one thing I know for sure, with no doubt in my mind, is that I want to be with you.' She took a breath. This was hard. *What if he didn't feel the same?* 'And if you don't feel the same, you need to tell me. I'm not playing games and I won't pretend. I'm twenty-six and I know what I want.' She stopped then, watching his face carefully. He was processing, finding the right words. She knew him well enough to know that.

Jamie turned towards her. He put his hands on her waist and pulled her onto his lap. 'Debbie Webb,

I love you. I want you here with me, always. I've been waiting for you, for a long time. But I never wanted to force your hand.' He held her close, then released her. Bob was frowning from the bar. He picked up his drink, downing it quickly. Debbie had hardly touched hers. 'Walk with me Debbie, the temperature has dropped slightly out there.'

6

His head was spinning, she'd come home for him. He was elated. She'd called him a neanderthal, and frankly, he felt like one too. He wanted to drag her off to a cave and make love to her. But he didn't. He held her hand and they strolled across the street to the bank building. It was after five and the gift shop was closed.

They peered through the window of the untenanted shop. Debbie let go of his hand and walked the length of the building, down the side lane. He followed her, curious to see her so excited.

'Look Jamie, this side opens up. It's a whole wall of bi-fold cedar and glass doors. And you can see, in there, how long the counter is. And there's a kitchen behind, I'm sure. Douglas Barlow is very clever, he has it set it up almost ready to go.' She turned to him then. 'How big is the space, do you think? Can you work it out?'

'Sure. I can give you a rough measurement.' He let her hand go and paced from the end of the building in the side lane to the front, and across to the front door. 'About six by fourteen metres, but I think the kitchen might tuck in behind the florist there, that shop doesn't go all the way back. Or perhaps room for cool rooms and so on. Around 84 – 100 square metres, I'd guess.'

Debbie's eyes had lit up. 'And the alfresco out here, that's another thirty or forty!' she turned on the spot, radiating enthusiasm.

'Is this what you want to do Debbie? A café? Not physiotherapy?' He was curious yet delighted to see her so happy.

'Yes! Ten times over, yes. I'd love to open a coffee shop.' She stopped, beaming from ear to ear. 'I think I told you already, in London. *Coffee is my calling.*'

'You did. I know nothing about coffee shops, running costs and so on, but I expect you do. First step, drop in to see Douglas Barlow tomorrow and ask what the rent is. Then do your numbers Deb.'

'I will. Oh, I will!' She spun again. 'There was a business element to my degree, you know for those wanting to set up a private practice. I know how to do a basic business plan and budget, and I understand the running costs from my café job in London. I was doing a lot of the ordering, rostering, and payroll there in the end.' She held his hand, tugging him around to the side of the building again. After peering through the glass doors, she turned back to him. 'And there's Dad. I'm sure he'll help me with the budget, the figures, to get a loan to complete the fit out. And I have some savings. Was going to buy a car with it, but I can walk from home to here, no problem.'

She pulled him further into the laneway, away from the street lights. 'Kiss me Jamie Tait. I've waited months. Kiss me now.'

Jamie gathered her in his arms, turning his back to the street, in case anyone walked by, and kissed her thoroughly. Finally, they pulled apart.

'We need to stop Debbie, or we're going to be booked for indecency in public.' He laughed. He could wait until they had some privacy. She was his, that was enough, in the moment.

She pouted and he kissed her lips. Debbie pulled him closer, gave a little moan in his ear. 'We need. To consummate. This. Us.' She breathed against his jaw. 'Very, very soon.'

He straightened. His jeans were uncomfortable. Holding her tightly, he growled in her ear. 'I have every intention. To consummate. But not here. Not like this. We need privacy, and time. I'll make it happen.' She melted against him, making sexy little mewling noises. It was all he could do not to find a darker place, right here in town.

He gently pulled away from her, then tucked her arm through his. 'I'm taking you home now, and I will see you tomorrow. Would you like me to come to see Douglas with you?'

Debbie's face was surprised. 'Thank you, but no. This is something I'd like to do on my own. I'll speak to Douglas, do my sums, then talk to you further. And Dad. It might take a few days, so please don't say anything to your parents or Greg just yet. In case it's not do-able for me.'

They were back at his car, in front of the pub. 'I'll drive you home.' He opened the door for her, then slipped in the other side. 'But Deb, if it isn't do-able, as you say, what will you do? Will you still stay?'

She chuckled. 'Of course I'll stay. I'll find work, no problem. Maybe like London, a bit of physio and some hospitality. A café is my dream, but if not now, then later.'

He relaxed. Debbie asked him if he'd like to

come in, but he could see she wanted to start on her research and talk to her dad. Another lingering kiss and she stepped out of the car. He was tingling, he'd have to work something out. For the first time, still living in the homestead with his parents seemed limiting.

'See you at the barbecue tomorrow. Love you.' She waved as he drove off.

7

Although she was bursting to discuss the café idea with her parents, and her news about staying. And Jamie Tait. Mostly Jamie Tait. Debbie wanted to hold the buzz she was feeling to herself overnight. She ate dinner with her parents, her mum chatting about the trip to Spain she wanted to do the following year. Debbie dropped a couple of hints that she may not be in London then, and saw her dad raise his eyebrows, but her mum seemed to disregard her comments altogether.

She went to her room early, feigning tiredness, and opened her laptop. She made a list of things to do, with regard to the café idea, including speaking with Douglas Barlow and writing a business plan. She decided she'd see Douglas first thing in the morning, if he was free, and then talk to her father.

The other thing on her mind was Jamie. And how they could be together. He still lived at home, although the homestead was huge. Would he want her to move in there? Would she be comfortable doing that? She really wanted to make a home with Jamie, as soon as possible, but she had to be realistic. Paying a lot of rent wouldn't work and he needed to be on or near the farm. They'd talk about it, in the next few weeks. Jamie was a thinker, he'd be working on it too, she was sure.

NEXT MORNING, SHE WAS SHOWERED AND DRESSED and had omelettes cooking for breakfast, when her parents appeared.

'What's this? Something smells delicious.' Her mum came through, hugged Debbie briefly and flicked the switch on the kettle. She called out, looking over her shoulder, 'Steve! Debbie has breakfast made! It's ready!'

'Don't rush him, this can keep.' Debbie checked

the bacon, turning the heat down, but her dad appeared as she spoke.

'Good morning love.' He kissed the top of her head. 'I smell bacon.'

Debbie giggled. 'It's ready if you are. Have a seat and I'll serve it up.'

'Wow!' Her mum turned her plate slightly. 'It looks as good as it smells. You've got a real knack Deb.'

'Thanks Mum.'

Her father didn't speak until he'd finished his omelette, then he sat back and rubbed his tummy. 'Best omelette ever love.' He reached for his tea, 'what are your plans today?'

I'm going to run some errands this morning and get the fixings for salad and dessert. Then I'll bake this afternoon and help mum prepare for the barbecue.'

'Oh good.' Her mum stood, clearing the plates as she spoke. 'Take my car and pick up whatever you think we might need. They're bringing the meat, so just salads and dessert. I can tidy up while you do that.' She turned to her husband. 'Do you think the back yard needs a quick mow, Steve?'

'No. it's short enough, but dry. I'd love to water it, but we can't with the drought. Best to leave it as it is.

I can set the outdoor furniture up, and give it all a wipe Rach, if that helps.'

Debbie watched her mum stand back, hands on hips. She nodded, then clapped her hands. 'Good. We've all got jobs to do. Thank you for breakfast Deb, lovely of you.' She patted her own tummy, 'but don't do it every day, will you?'

Debbie laughed. 'No, it's a treat. Thank you for having me.' She picked up her mum's car keys. 'Alright, if you don't mind washing up, I'll make a start on the shopping.'

Debbie parked behind the supermarket and walked through to the main street, standing at the front of the old bank building at eight-thirty. The florist had just opened and was setting buckets of flowers and a small table of giftware just outside the door. Debbie glanced at her watch.

'If you're waiting for Barlow's, they park in back. It's likely they're already here. Just try the door.' The woman smiled as she spoke.

Debbie smiled back and turned the door knob. It opened. She waved to the florist as she ducked inside. The staircase rose up through the centre, just as she remembered when her father was the bank manager. She ran quickly up the stairs, her espadrilles making a light tap on each tread as she went. She had on the maxi skirt from last night, an abstract pattern in soft blue, and a crisp white blouse with no sleeves, tucked in. At the top of the stairs she pushed open a solid rosewood door, with a plaque reading *Douglas Barlow, Solicitor* in its centre.

The reception area was large and light-filled, the high ceilings creating a cool interior. Jamie's mum was right, it was beautiful. She walked across the dark green Axminster carpet to the reception desk. There was no one there. She cleared her throat and Frances Barlow popped out through a door to the left, a cup of tea in her hand.

'Oh hello. Sorry, I didn't hear you come in.' She set the tea on the desk, then paused, looking at Debbie over her glasses. A petite woman, somewhere near sixty, she was just as Debbie remembered.

'Goodness! Debbie Webb! I didn't recognise you at first. Hello.' Frances smiled and came around the desk.

'Hello Mrs Barlow. I don't have an appointment, but I was hoping I could speak with Mr Barlow before his day started properly.'

'Please, you're an adult now. Call me Frances.' She returned to the desk and picked up the cup of tea. 'I was just taking this in to Douglas and he doesn't have an appointment until ten, so come on through.'

Debbie followed Frances in and was greeted warmly by Douglas, also insisting she use his first name. They chatted for a moment, about her being home from London and how pleased her parents must be, then the phone rang, and Frances returned to the outer office.

'Have a seat Debbie. What can I do for you.' Douglas took a sip of his tea. 'Would you like one? Frances won't be long.'

'Thank you Mr Barlow, er Douglas, but I've just had one at home.' Debbie tried to relax. 'I wanted to ask you about the tenancy downstairs. The empty one. The café.' Now she was rambling, and she took a breath. 'I'd like to know your plans for it, the lease amount and terms, and if possible to inspect the premises to understand what is already there, and what needs to be done to complete the fit out.' She waited, her hands trembled slightly. Anticipation. Fear of disappointment.

Douglas leaned forward. 'Are you interested in it for yourself Debbie? I recall that you were working in the medical field.'

'I was. I'm a physiotherapist. I've been working in a hospital in London for just over five years. But wages were low, when I started, so I took a job with a café to help make ends meet. For the last eighteen months I've worked more hours at the café each week than the hospital. By choice.' She warmed to her subject. 'I love it. So much. The busy-ness of the work, the customers, the other staff. I became a manager too and was involved in rosters, ordering, some marketing. The owner never really got on board with social media, so I managed that too. And coffee. I love coffee. All types of coffee. And cakes and snacks. Making them, I mean.' She noticed then that he'd leaned back, his fingers steepled under his chin, just nodding for her to continue, or elaborate.

'So you're home now Debbie. Barrington is where you want to be?'

'I am. I um, came home because I was ready, it was time. And...' She wasn't sure if she should discuss her personal situation in what was, ostensibly, a business discussion.

'And.' He prompted.

Alright, she thought. It makes a difference. Gives me stability, for a landlord. 'And for Jamie Tait.' She lifted her chin a little, her cheeks warmed by the admission. 'We, um, have an understanding. He's, er, supportive of my dream to have a café.' She rushed on. 'But this is just me. He's not financing. I'm writing a business plan, and once I know all the figures I'll work out a budget. Dad will help. And I'll get a business loan.' She was rambling again, and she could hear the inexperience in her words, and felt the opportunity slipping away from her.

Douglas stood. Debbie's heart sank. 'It's one hundred and twenty-four square metres. Most of the fit-out is completed, I have installed a cool room and walk in freezer, ovens and so one. I had good advice from the fit-out people, a group that usually do places in Melbourne. Because that's what we need here. The town is ready, despite what some locals say. But it needs furnishings, plate ware, cutlery, cookware. Come with me, let's take a look, we can chat as we go.'

Feeling giddy with excitement, she followed him down the back stairs, where he opened the back entrance to the café and took her through the store-room area, kitchen and then out to the counter.

'I was going to get a coffee machine. You know the coffee companies will provide one if you use their coffee? But I don't know coffee well enough, and I thought a tenant may have a preference.' He leaned against the counter. 'What do you think Debbie?'

'It's beautiful, you've done such a great job, the

layout is perfect.' She clapped her hands. 'But is it within my reach?'

'Well, I'm playing the long game here Debbie. I want a well-run café that brings the main street into the twenty-first century. I can offer you free rent for the first three months, giving you time to get started. Then half rent for a further nine months.' He handed her the set of keys. 'Stay here, have a really good look around. I'll go up, I have a meeting to prepare for. In fact, hang on to the keys until you've spoken to your father, and Jamie. Bring him in to have a look. Today, tomorrow. Take a few days to see if you can make it work, then let me know your thoughts.'

Debbie looked at the keys in her hand. 'Are you sure Douglas? I know I'm young and haven't owned a business. But I have café experience. And I'll work hard.'

'Debbie, you're exactly the type of tenant I was hoping for. You know this town and its people, and you have experience. London experience. Combine that with youth and a good work ethic. You'll do well, Debbie. Have a good look around, make some notes. Then talk to your father.' He held out his hand. Debbie shook it, her shoulders back and head high. Douglas believed in her. If her dad could help organise the finance she needed, she could do this.

'Thank you Douglas. I will do that. I'll bring the keys back the day after tomorrow and we'll speak again.'

'I look forward to it.'

8

Wheeling his stockhorse to the left, Jamie cantered after the yearling bull that seemed determined to return to the larger herd. Cody was a young horse, but Jamie grinned when he fearlessly leaned in to the bull and turned it. Only three years old, the chestnut gelding was proving himself today. Slowing to a fast walk, they settled in behind the mob they were pushing along the laneway towards the main yards. It was noisy, dogs barking, and Greg was tearing around on a motorbike while their dad had gone ahead on the quad-bike to block the hayshed area – it wouldn't take much for the bulls to push past the temporary fencing around the freshly-baled lucerne – but his young horse was focussed on the job at hand. Greg appeared beside them, one of the cattle dogs on the back of the bike, grinning broadly.

Jamie laughed. 'Just like the old days, hey brother?' Greg gave him a thumbs up. On days like today, Jamie could see them working the farm together. Greg only became obnoxious when he drank. Maybe he *would* come home and settle.

They moved past the shearing shed, then the original manager's house. Jamie steadied Cody, then turned towards the old cottage. They'd had a manager in it when the boys were young, but once Jamie declared he'd be staying on the farm, old Geoffrey retired. Vacant now, they used it occasionally for over-flow accommodation and lately his mum had suggested turning it into short term accommodation, but his dad wasn't keen to have strangers around the stock. He'd always thought Jamie or Greg would move in there when one of them married.

Greg called out, pointing at a beast that had broken away from the herd and Jamie cantered Cody to retrieve it. The image of the cottage stuck in his mind as pushed the cattle forward. It was probably around one hundred years old but had always been a worker's cottage, so it didn't have the flashy features of the main homestead, the pressed-metal ceilings, and wide verandas. But it was solid and had potential. No garden to speak of either, although it had a fenced yard, a carport, and an orchard at the back. He could talk to Debbie, see if she thought it would do them, to begin with. He rose in his stirrups, waving to where his father now sat on the top rail of the yards, new Vet Angus Hamilton beside him. His father waved back, then disappeared. He'd have everything ready to drench the mob when they got there, and they'd separate the ones going in to the saleyards the next day.

GREG LEANED ON THE BATHROOM DOORJAMB, watching Jamie shave. He was already dressed, he'd showered first and taken most of the hot water. Jamie didn't care, he was seeing Debbie and that's all he could think about.

He glanced at his brother. 'Who are you trying to impress? It's just dinner at the Webs.' Greg was wearing crisp jeans, fancy runners, and an open neck-shirt that Jamie suspected was a designer label.

'I'm just coming for dinner. Going out afterwards.' Greg straightened, ran his fingers through his hair, then sauntered away.

'Going out? Where? The pub closes at eleven.' Jamie called out, he was curious. Greg was dressed for a date, but who would he be seeing here in Barrington?

'You never know your luck. In a small town.' Greg called back, over his shoulder. 'But it looks like you're sorted, with gorgeous Debbie.'

Jamie grinned. 'I am sorted. And don't you forget it big brother.' He walked into his room after another quick look in the bathroom mirror. His own hair could do with a trim, and he'd taken off his light stubble. He hoped for some time alone with Debbie and didn't want to give her pash-rash. He pulled on his best jeans, riding boots and a blue checked shirt. He didn't need fancy clothes to impress his girl.

He joined his parents in the kitchen. They were ready, his dad had the meat in an esky and his mum carried a bottle of wine.

'Greg's gone ahead, said he might leave early and catch up with some mates at the pub.' Jill handed a small bag to him, with jars of something inside. 'Homemade tomato relish, Debbie used to love it.'

He'd wanted to take his own car, so he and Debbie could slip away afterwards. Maybe bring her back here to look at the manager's cottage. But he knew his parents would enjoy having a drink with Debbie's folks.

'I'll drive your car mum, and we can all go together.' Jamie reached for the keys on the kitchen table.

'Thank you son.' Ross Tait was a man of few words.

DEBBIE RAN OUT TO MEET GREET THEM AS SOON AS they pulled up. Her hair was loose around her shoulders. Jamie vaguely noted she had on a shorter outfit than the night before, but his eyes never left hers.

'Debbie looks well.' Jill's tone was dry. He glanced at his mother, she had that *I'm your mother and I know what you're up* to look. He chuckled. Never could get anything past his mum.

'You go ahead son, we'll bring our stuff in.' His father's tone sounded amused. Jamie saw a look pass between his parents. They knew. His mum had always known, but he realised now they'd probably spoken about it. Debbie coming home. They liked her, always had and he knew they'd be happy for him. For them.

'SHOULD WE WAIT FOR GREG? THE MEAT'S ALMOST done.' Steve spoke to Jill, but Ross answered.

His tone was gruff. 'No, thanks Steve. He should be here, not sure where he's gotten to, Jill's left two messages. If the meat is ready, we'll start.'

Jamie was surprised Greg hadn't been at the Webb's when they arrived, but also secretly pleased, it had been lovely with just the six of them. He and Debbie had held hands under the table, and she'd pressed her thigh against his, more than once.

They'd only just started when Greg's noisy car pulled up outside. Rachel pushed her chair back and rushed to let him in.

They heard Greg's deep voice as she opened the door. 'Rachel, you could be Debbie's sister, not her mother.' Jamie frowned, Greg sounded drunk. Rachel giggled and led him through to the back deck.

'You're late son, you should apologise to Rachel and Steve.' Ross was not impressed.

'So sorry, I got caught up with the lads and lost track.' Greg grinned at them all, reached over and shook Steve's hand. 'Looks delicious.' Rachel handed him a plate and he filled it with meat and salad, making small talk as he did.

Typical Greg. Throws them a smile and all is forgiven.

Jamie wasn't buying the story about being at the pub. His brother had a few drinks under his belt, sure enough, but he also looked a bit *crumpled*, not crisp and neat like he was earlier. Jamie passed the salad dressing to him and caught a faint whiff of perfume. *Greg had been with a woman. Who?*

Ross and Steve began talking about the economy and the drought, and how small towns like Barrington were suffering. With the rivers low, tourism was down, and a lot of the main street businesses were struggling. Jamie watched as Debbie joined the conversation, asking questions about business, and what it would take to turn the economy around. Jamie knew then that she had seen Douglas Barlow, maybe even looked at the café. They'd talk about it later.

Greg engaged Jill in a conversation about football. Mostly off-field gossip and his mum chatted with Debbie about London. Jamie was happy to just sit at the table, his leg touching Debbie's, listening to her speak. She'd matured, of course, but she was still the lovely warm-hearted girl he'd known since early school days.

He helped Debbie and Rachel clear their main course plates before Jill popped into the kitchen to get the desserts out of the fridge. He went back to the men then, Steve was asking Greg when he was going to give up football and come home.

Leaning back in his chair, Greg nodded towards Jamie. 'After this season ends, I think Steve. I'm carrying a few niggling injuries and working with little brother on the farm today made me realise just how much I miss the lifestyle here.' Jamie was surprised, but he could see his brother's words had hit a chord with his dad, who almost cracked a smile. Jamie wasn't sure what he thought. If Greg came home and *really shared* the workload, it would be great. They could build the herd back up once rain came, improve the pastures, maybe even buy more land. But he some residual doubt that Greg would be content in Barrington. Unless he was seeing someone local, had a relationship here.

His parents made a move to leave, after dessert and coffee, and Jamie stood, ready to take them home.

'Mate. Stay here and have another drink with

Debbie. I'll take mum and dad home.' Greg grinned at him.

'How much have you had to drink tonight Greg?' Jill looked uncertain.

'I doubt I'm over the limit, don't worry mum.'

Jamie's instinct was to step in, drive them home, but his desire to stay a bit longer with Debbie held sway.

Ross spoke up. 'I'll drive. I'm okay.' He turned to Greg. 'Give me your keys Greg, Jamie can bring our car home later.' Jamie breathed a sigh of relief.

9

Standing at the front gate with Jamie and her parents, she waved as Ross, Jill and Greg pulled away from the kerb. Her hand was in Jamie's, and she wanted to get him alone to talk about the café.

'We're going to turn in now Deb. I've already put the dishwasher on.' Rachel nudged Steve.

'Oh yes. Goodnight you two.' He shook Jamie's hand. 'Thanks for coming over.' He kissed Debbie on the cheek and followed Rachel inside.

Jamie's hand tightened in hers and as soon as the front door closed he pulled her into his arms, kissing her deeply. She felt herself melt against him, then leaned back, her hands pressed against his chest. She saw the confusion in his eyes.

'First things first, cowboy.' Her tone was light, teasing.

'Your mum just said the dishes are done.' His tone was light too, and she appreciated that he *got* her.

'I do want to kiss you, really I do. And more. But I need to talk to you first.' Debbie was bubbling over with excitement. She'd spent a couple of hours developing a budget and outlining a business plan. She'd talk to her dad in the morning, but she was sure she could open the café with a business loan, smaller than she'd imagined. With her own savings to complete the fit-out – buying the kitchen equipment and furniture – she'd just need a loan to cover initial operating costs.

'Alright. Talk to me.' Jamie wrapped his arms around her again, but instead of kissing her mouth he just pecked the tip of her nose. 'What is this conversation we need to have that's more urgent than, well, kissing?' He quirked one eyebrow up and Debbie laughed, then covered her mouth.

'Ssh. I don't want to wake mum and dad up but come back inside. We can sit in the kitchen, close the door.' Debbie almost dragged him back to the front door, opened it quietly and ushered him into the kitchen.

'There's a bottle of Baileys on the sideboard, and some Grandfather Port. Pour us a drink each and I'll just get my laptop.' Debbie scooted back to her room, grabbed her laptop, and returned in moments.

With the laptop open, she went over the discussion with Douglas Barlow and the terms of the lease. Then she shared her spreadsheet, how much she'd budgeted to get started. How the loan she needed was smaller than she'd expected.

Watching his face carefully, as he digested her plans, she hoped he would be supportive. She needed him to be behind her, one hundred percent.

'You've done your homework Deb, in just a few hours. And I can see you have a real handle on what's needed. But I have questions.' His tone was quiet, serious. But Debbie needed someone to ask the hard questions, make sure she'd thought of everything, before she spoke to her dad and the bank. Before she jumped in to her very first business.

'Okay. Ask.' She picked up a pen and pulled her notebook closer. She'd jot down anything Jamie thought she should include or had forgotten.

'Firstly, most importantly, what can I do to help?' Surprised she laid the pen down.

'Help? Jamie, I'm not asking for funds! I just need to know you're supportive, you know, emotionally.' She reached out, touching his hand with hers. Her voice firm, she continued, 'I need to do this myself, but I want to know you're okay with it. It will be long hours, weekends too.'

He grinned. 'Of course I'm with you on this. And Debbie, my work isn't nine-to-five either. I work long hours and weekends. I get it.' He picked up the Baileys, and she nodded as he put another shot in her glass.

'I do have a question about the current economic downturn, with the drought. Listening to the conversation tonight, do you think you'll be able to get traction while you're still in the no rent and low rent period?' Jamie leaned back slightly.

'I'm glad you asked. I've done some research and thought about that quite a bit. Starting a business in a low time, and surviving, bodes well for when the economy picks up. If I live cheaply, here, with mum and dad, and run it by myself initially, I think I can build it organically. Once I'm underway I will start marketing through social channels and I will speak to the tourism office here, see if I can put flyers in local accommodation places. Working together, collaboratively, yields results. I learned that in

London.' She could hear the confidence, and excitement, in her own voice and Jamie's face showed surprise, followed quickly by approval. It was a question she knew the bank would ask and she'd already written that piece into her business plan.

'Sounds good, Deb. Show me the list of stuff you will need to buy.' He leaned in again and she angled the computer screen so they could both see it.

'This list here, is kitchen equipment, crockery and so on. I will do a deal with a coffee company for the coffee machine.' She grinned at him. 'Douglas suggested that, and there are two brands I favour. Having really good coffee, you know *Melbourne style* coffee, will be a game changer.' She clicked to the next page of her list. 'I need furniture. Tables and chairs, maybe some benches. Indoor and outdoor. Potentially really expensive, but I remember this place in Notting Hill that was a bit quirky, had a lot of mismatched timber chairs, all painted bright colours. It's possible I could pick the furniture up second hand.'

'Second hand. Hmm. I know there are places doing it tough in this economy. Is there somewhere you could go to get furniture from businesses that have closed their doors? Like an auction house? You might pick up quality pieces for a fraction of their value.' Jamie's voice had risen a bit, he was enthusiastic, and she couldn't love him more, in that moment.

'That's a brilliant idea? I'll do some research. Maybe I can get most of the kitchen equipment that way too!' She wanted to jump online then and there and get started.

His arm snaked around her waist, and he pulled her onto his lap. 'There's time Deb. You don't have to do everything tonight. Will you talk to your dad about this?'

'Yes! In the morning. I want to take him, and mum too if she's interested, down to the café. I have the keys. Show them through. Then I'll go over the finances with dad. There'll be insurance and so on, I could use his guidance on all of that.' She kissed him then, hard on the mouth. His response was instant, he kissed her back, deeply. For a moment all thoughts of the café left her mind. Coming up for air, she took his face in her hands, nibbled his bottom lip, running the tip of her tongue over his lips.

'Debbie!' he growled. 'Don't start something you can't finish.'

She giggled. Tried the same move again, but he intercepted her.

'Actually, we need to talk about something else.' His tone was serious, so she stopped messing around, cocking her head on one side, waiting for him to continue.

'Us. We need some privacy. And as much as I'd like to race you off to your bedroom, I'm not comfortable, you know, *doing stuff* in your parents' house.' She nodded at his words.

'I know. But Jamie, I wouldn't be comfortable at your house either, *doing stuff.*' She chuckled, then took a breath. 'I can't afford rent, with the business. Not straight away. Maybe after a few months. I'm sorry, it would be easier if I took a job, rented my own place ...' She trailed off.

'How tired are you? I may have a solution. Would you like to come with me, have a look?' Jamie glanced at his watch as he spoke. 'I know it's late ...'

10

Debbie slid off his lap, grabbed his hand. 'Show me!' she demanded.

He didn't hesitate. 'Come with me.' Once outside, he opened the door of his mum's car, settling her, than almost ran to the driver's side, sliding in and starting the car in one swift movement.

Ten minutes later they reached the front gate to the farm. She turned to him, confused. 'But I thought?'

'Wait!' he said, driving beyond the gate for a further five hundred metres. He turned in, stopping at a second gate, grinning at her. 'The passenger has to open the gate.'

'Oh. Yes.' She leapt from the car, opened the gate

wide, holding it while he drove through, then closing it again before getting back in the car.

'You're a farmer's girlfriend alright, knowing to close any gate you open.' He held her hand as he drove slowly up the narrow driveway.

'You taught me well.' Was her only response, but she was leaning forward, peering through the windscreen. He manoeuvred around a pot hole, then dipped into a small valley. He stopped, the cottage sat neatly in the headlights, the front yard overgrown, and the side fence on a slight lean. He hoped it would be good enough, for a start.

He watched her, she didn't speak, just gazed at it for what felt like minutes. His heart sank, it certainly wasn't what she was used to. He was about to tell her his plans to fix it up, but she turned to him, eyes shining. 'Really? Here? We can live here? Together?' Turning away, she scrambled out of the car. 'Keep the car lights on, I want to have a closer look.'

Jamie chuckled, stepped out of the car and retrieved a torch from the trunk. He turned it on, then turned the car off. Taking her hand, he led her through the garden gate, up the overgrown path to the front door. It had a small front veranda. 'I could extend this.' She didn't say a word, but he felt her whole body pulsed with excitement.

He opened the front door, it wasn't locked. They stepped into a small hallway, a bedroom leading off each side, then walked through to a lounge area with an enclosed wood firebox. He shone the torch around. 'Ten-foot ceilings and all timber. Nothing fancy like the main homestead.' They stepped into the kitchen area. Small, it had been renovated about twenty years ago, but looked outdated now.

'Oh.' Her voice sounded tiny.

'We can re-do the kitchen Deb, it won't be like this for long.' Fear niggled at him again.

She spun around, threw her arms around his neck, and buried her face in his shoulder. She was crying. He patted her back. 'It's okay Deb, it was just a thought. We'll work something out.' She mumbled something against his chest.

'What was that?' He held her shoulders and gently moved her back so he could see her face, he'd placed the torch on the kitchen counter. Tears were streaming down her cheeks and his heart broke for her. The excitement of the café had been ruined by his badly thought-out plan to live here. He should have checked it out himself first, tidied it up a bit.

She sniffed, then looked up at him. 'I love you Jamie. This. House. Is.' She hiccupped. 'Perfect.' She stepped back, spun around. 'The kitchen is perfect.

Everything is perfect. I love it, I really love it! We can make this a home Jamie Tait.' He was stunned. Happy. Beyond happy.

Without thinking it through, he dropped to one knee. In the torchlight, he looked up at her, his own eyes wet. 'Marry me Debbie. Marry me. I've never been surer of anything in my life.'

She dropped to her knees in front of him, took his hands in hers and kissed them, one after the other. 'Yes! A million times yes!' Then she leapt into his arms, knocking them to the floor, her face hovering above his.

His mind was screaming *she said yes!* And *you're getting married!* As she lowered her lips to his.

11

Next morning, still elated from her night with Jamie, Debbie showered and joined her parents in the kitchen. With a coffee in front of her, she looked from one to the other, then grinned. 'We need to talk.'

Her mum's eyes narrowed. 'I heard you come in just before dawn young lady. Yes, we do need to talk.' Debbie saw her mum glance at her dad, then back to her. 'You know Jamie will never leave the farm? How are you ever going to have a relationship, with you in London?'

'Good question mum. I'm not going back to London. I've quit my jobs, I'm home for good. Well, for good, and for Jamie Tait.' She waited while her words sank in. Her dad seemed to get it first, as a slow smile spread across his features.

'Home. Here in Barrington? For good you say?' He held out his arms and she snuggled against his chest, murmuring, 'yes Dad.'

'No more London?' Rachel still seemed confused.

'No mum. I love Jamie. I've travelled and worked overseas. I'm ready to settle. Here. In Barrington.' Debbie said the words gently, but firmly.

'Jamie Tait.' Rachel looked at Steve. 'It was always Jamie Tait.' Steve nodded.

Debbie watched her mum stand and reach her hand out. Debbie took it, they were face to face. 'Oh Debbie!' And then her mum was crying, and Steve joined them, an arm around them both. 'I'm so happy for you darling. Jamie is.' She wiped her eyes. 'Perfect for you.'

Relieved, Debbie squeezed them both. She wanted to tell them he'd proposed, but they decided last night they'd tell all the parents together in a few days. Jamie wanted her to drive to the coast with him, choose a ring first.

'And there's something else. I want to open a café. In the shop at the old bank.' Debbie took a deep breath. 'I saw Douglas Barlow yesterday, I've started a business plan and Dad.' She stood on tiptoes, kissing him on the cheek. 'I'd like your advice. I'll need a small bank loan, not as much as I first thought, but I'd like you to check my projections before I go further.'

Looking at her mum again, she said, 'What do you think mum? I have the keys, would you and Dad like to come and see inside? Then I can talk you through my plans.'

Rachel threw back her head and laughed. 'Debbie, haven't I always told you that *girls can do anything*? Of course I want to come and see it! And I want to help. I can cook you know. Even if it's just while you're starting ...'

BY THE END OF THE NEXT WEEK SHE HAD A BUSINESS loan. Her parents had offered to help financially, but Debbie was determined to do this on her own, and she had signed the lease. She'd already begun ordering equipment, and Jamie had taken her to Newcastle to a couple of auctions, picking up a lot of items, including the furniture, way below cost.

The following Friday night she invited a small group to the café. It wouldn't open for another four weeks, but she had furniture. She was there with her parents, and Jamie and his parents. Greg had returned to Sydney, he was playing the next day. Douglas and Frances Barlow joined them, and Greta from the florist. Jamie's mates Ben Evans and Drum Murray were there, and the new Vet, Angus Hamilton.

Jamie and Steve opened bottles of champagne and Rachel and Jill passed the glasses around.

'A toast!' Jamie raised his glass. 'To Debbie and ...' He looked at her. 'Do you have a name picked out Debbie, for the café?'

'Oh. I don't know. I should ...' She trailed off.

'Just wait.' Jamie handed his glass to Ben and disappeared inside the kitchen for a minute. He returned, carrying an enormous parcel. Big, but flat. It was wrapped in brown paper. 'I got you something. You know, for the opening.' He was grinning so broadly, Debbie looked around the faces. Jill and Ross Tait looked smug. They knew what it was. Everyone else was as clueless as she was.

Stepping forward, she began removing the brown paper. Something pink and white inside, with writing. She couldn't read it all. But it was a sign. A very *big* sign. Excited, she tore the rest of the paper off in a frenzy, then stood back. The sign was beautiful. In white italics it said *Coffee is my Calling* on a bright pink background, then Debbie Webb to one side, smaller. She flew into Jamie's arms, Ben and Steve quickly grabbing the sign to stop it falling over.

'It's perfect! You're perfect! But how did you know?' She turned then, the whole group was laughing.

Her dad was bent over, laughing so hard that Ross had to bang him on the back a couple of times. 'How many times have I heard you tell me, and others, just that? *Coffee is my Calling.* Debbie, you say it with such conviction, it *is the perfect name.*'

Debbie giggled, looked around. 'It really is. My calling. Coffee.'

Amidst the laughter, Jamie cleared his throat. 'There's, er, something else.' Debbie knew what he was about to do, and just stood, waiting. In moments the room was silent. He dropped to one knee, holding the ring box out to Debbie. 'I've already asked, and you've said yes. But Debbie, tonight, in front of our families and friends, I want to confirm my commitment. Debbie Webb, will you marry me?'

She nodded, trying not to cry as he slid the ring on to her finger. The room erupted, everyone laughing and talking and jostling to congratulate them, but in that instant, as he slid the ring on and she nodded her agreement, her eyes locked on his, time stood still. They were encased in a bubble of happiness that she'd never, ever forget.

THE END

ABOUT THE AUTHOR
SUSAN MACKIE

A voracious reader, Susan dreamed of becoming a writer from the age of eight. Career advisors told her it wasn't a real thing and suggested journalism. So she became a journalist, then took a zig-zag path to publish her first book in 2020, via a varied career in publishing, marketing, tourism and small business. Susan even worked in State Government for a few years (but she doesn't talk about that much).

Nervous about the release of Charlie's Will, she told Bloke while sitting on the sofa one night, that she'd be happy if she sold fifty. Charlie's Will quickly reached Number One in its genre on Amazon - motivating Susan to crack on with more stories and take her writing seriously. Finally. Now Susan is a happy Indie Publisher and offers services to other writers (editing, formatting). She is also the publisher of the Love in a Sunburnt Land Anthology series, co-authored with four (quite brilliant) Aussie women.

Susan loves engaging with fellow authors and readers, and she discovered something she thought was kinda funny. A lot of authors tell her they're introverted. It's a writerly thing, apparently. But (and here's the funny bit), Susan isn't. Introverted. Not one bit. Not at all. Speaking and presenting at writers festivals, conferences and libraries is totally her thing.

So it's okay to send Susan a message, ask a question and chat on social media. She thrives on it and will always respond. Send her a photo of one of her books 'in the wild' and she'll share it. Everywhere.

https://susanmackie.com/

ALSO BY SUSAN MACKIE

Charlie's Will - Barrington Book 1

A Place to Start Over - Barrington Book 2

Love in the Ragged Mountain Ranges - Barrington Book 3 (novella)

The Bee Whisperer - Barrington Book 4

Meggie & Max - Barrington Book 5 (novella)

Something in the Water - Barrington Book 6 (novella)

* 9 7 9 8 2 1 5 8 3 4 9 4 7 *